Our

~~OAKEN'S~~ BOOK

FOR THE RECORDING

OF ~~INVENTIONS~~

Adventure!

Adventure NOTEBOOK

By Elsa

Kristoff and Anna

with help from Becky Matheson
and Jessica Julius

Disney PRESS
Los Angeles • New York

This Label Applies to Text Stock Only

Official kingdom of Arendelle documentation information

Editorial by Eric Geron Design by Lindsay Broderick
A special thank you to Mike and Lori for all their artistry.

For information address Disney Press,
1101 Flower Street, Glendale, California 91201.

Printed in the United States of America
First Hardcover Edition, November 2016
1 3 5 7 9 10 8 6 4 2

FAC-008598-16260
ISBN 978-1-4847-8662-8

Library of Congress Control Number: 2016939524

For more Disney Press fun,
visit www.disneybooks.com

Hello, Arendelle! Anna here! I have some very exciting and important kingdom news! Elsa, Kristoff, Sven, Olaf, and I are heading to Troll Valley for the annual Crystal Ceremony!

It's a special honor to be invited to the Crystal Ceremony, where Grand Pabbie, the wise and kind troll leader, honors all the young trolls who have earned their level-one crystals. The ceremony takes place under the Northern Lights, and Kristoff's entire family is going to be there. Elsa and I can't wait to learn more about the trolls and their tradition.

We just stopped into Oaken's Trading Post and Sauna to pick up carrots for Sven before we head off. (Sven can never get enough carrots. And Kristoff likes them, too.) I asked Oaken for a notebook, but all of his had already been sold. I thought we were out of luck . . . until Oaken pulled this one from a drawer! It's slightly worn, and Oaken said he doodled some ideas for his inventions on a few of the pages, but that just adds character. I dusted it off and said we'd take it. It'll be perfect for documenting the trolls' special Crystal Ceremony for the official "History of Arendelle" records. And who knows—maybe we'll even use it to jot down a few of our adventures along the way.

After all, I have a feeling this trip is going to be full of surprises!

Good-bye, Oaken's Trading Post and Sauna. Troll Valley, here we come!

I am so thrilled to spend time with Anna!

Seeing the annual Crystal Ceremony in Troll Valley will be simply amazing.

But an exciting new adventure with my sister?

Even better.

Olaf says,
"Hi, everyone!"
He thought this book needed pictures . . .
so he added his own special touch.

Not really sure what I'm supposed to do with this, but Anna asked me to write in here, so . . . hello, Arendelle?

Sven and I are taking Anna, Elsa, and Olaf to see the Crystal Ceremony. It's a very important tradition in my family. Everyone's going to be there, including Grand Pabbie and Bulda. They'll be so happy when we arrive.

SVEN SAYS, "I miss BULDA'S CARROT CAKE." I do too, buddy.

"WE should have brought MORE CARROTS."

Before we continue our trek up to Troll Valley, we'll tell you a little about ourselves!

Elsa

My big sister, who is magical in every way.

She loves winter and is never bothered by the cold.

SHE'S A GENIUS WITH ICE.

But most importantly, she's my best friend.

Olaf

Elsa created Olaf. He reminds us both of when we were kids.

HIS FAVORITE SEASON IS SUMMER.

And he likes warm hugs!

Anna

drawn by Elsa

My little sister, who has quite the sense of adventure!

YEAH, SHE'S ALWAYS TRYING TO CLIMB A MOUNTAIN.

. . . OR JUMP IN A RIVER.

. . . or in front of a sword!

SHE ALWAYS FOLLOWS HER HEART.

Because she's fearless and brave.

YEAH, SHE IS.

Kristoff

The best ice harvester and deliverer in all of Arendelle!

His best friend is Sven.

He's always a little smelly, but I don't mind.

He makes Anna really happy.

Elsa! Okay, she's right. He does.

drawn by Anna

SVEN

DRAWN by KRISTOFF

SVEN SAYS, "I'M THE BEST REINDEER EVER. I LOVE CARROTS AND LONG WALKS IN THE SNOW."

Olaf says that Sven loves trying to "kiss" his nose.

CHART FOR RECORDING OF

SEPTEMBER

SUN	MON	TUE	WED	THU	FRI	SAT
					1	2
3	4	5	6	7	8	9
10	11	12	13	14	15	16
17	18	19	20	21	22	23
24	25	26	27	28	29	30

It's one of Oaken's notes! It looks like he was tracking the Northern Lights activity in Arendelle.

THE NORTHERN LIGHTS

BY OAKEN

OCTOBER

SUN	MON	TUE	WED	THU	FRI	SAT
1	2	3	4	5	6	7
8	9	10	11	12	13	14
15	16	17	18	19	20	21
22	23	24	25	26	27	28
29	30	31				

THE NORTHERN LIGHTS WERE EXTRA BRIGHT HERE!

According to his chart, it's been a while since the Northern Lights last appeared. Do you think they will be back by the night of the Crystal Ceremony?

I hope so! We can ask Bulda when we reach Troll Valley.

Hoo-hoo!

I love inventing new things that people will enjoy

The Creators Contest is almost here!

But uff da! Inventor's block does not give me good feelings.

"Always watch for the silver lining. . . "

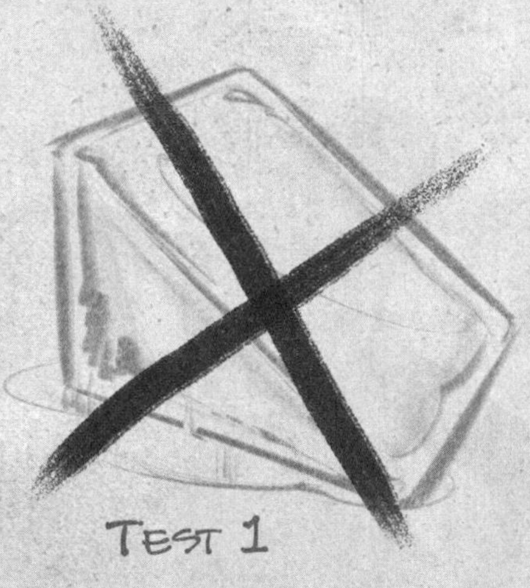

Ice Lantern

My inventor's block is cured!
A lantern for the temporary
capturing of the polar signals.

I really love when the Northern Lights are out. The colors are like a shimmering rainbow of happiness. Olaf thinks they are a giant sky party!

But there's no party tonight. The sky is dark and the lights aren't shining.

Olaf wanted to know if the Northern Lights were stolen by an evil sky monster.

I told him not to worry and that maybe it's just not quite cold enough out.

OR maybe a sky reindeer thought they were sparkly sky carrots and ate them all. Let's ask Sven.

Sven says don't be ridiculous.

Hey! I'm the only one who can talk for Sven.

Sven says that's not true.

Does the season affect the Northern Lights

No, but the Northern Lights do tend to look brighter in the autumn and winter because it's darker out.

Will the ceremony still go on if the Northern Lights don't appear?
I don't know. It's never happened before.

A GUIDE TO SVEN'S NOISES

BY KRISTOFF

ARRRRUUUUUKKKKKK = "Let's go back to Oaken's for more carrots."

RURURURURURURURU = "Carrots are delicious."

GUHHHHHHHHHHHHH = "Where did all the carrots go?"

CRUNCHCRUNCHCRUNCH = "This carrot is perfect."

MMMMMMMMMMMMMMM = "Let's just live in a carrot garden."

AAAAYYYYYYYUUUUUUU = "Thank you, Kristoff! You're my best friend."

Note to Self: Might need to hide the carrots. They're going fast.

Sven didn't
like that idea.

It's a good thing we stopped at Oaken's! This notebook is already filling up with useful information. Oaken also gave us a special "super-strong rope of his own invention." Kristoff is right that it looks like any ordinary rope, but Oaken says it can hold or pull almost anything. I don't know what we'll use it for, but I'm sure it will be good to have as we continue up into the mountains!

I have all the winter gear we could ever need. I live in the mountains!

The rope really doesn't seem all that super, but Anna likes Oaken's inventions.

We're almost at the top of the mountain. Troll Valley's not far from here!

Kristoff has been telling us all about the Crystal Ceremony on our trek. He says this celebration is meant to signify the relationship that the trolls have with nature. It sounds like it's a beautiful sight to witness!

THEY TAKE CARE OF IT, AND IT TAKES CARE OF THEM.

We've stopped for a moment at the top of the mountain. We should be with my family soon! Ahhh . . . I always like when the trail on the other side of the mountain gives way to the steaming vents and birch trees. It may look like jagged cliffs overlooking any old valley, but this valley is actually pretty special. I can't wait to see Bulda and the others.

TROLL VALLEY

We're in Troll Valley! The moment we arrived, there was a sudden change in the air, and then the trolls rolled out from every corner of the valley to greet us!

I asked Bulda when the Crystal Ceremony will start, and she said—wait, what was it again?

WE GUARDIANS of EARTH do KNOW
Autumn lights AND CRYSTALS glow
So OUR bond MAY DEEPEN AND GROW.

I'm still not quite sure what that means.

I don't really know, either. Troll wisdom is very confusing.

Kristoff?

Bulda is saying that the Crystal Ceremony has to be performed during autumn, which ends in three nights. I want to talk to Grand Pabbie about the ceremony, but he isn't here. I'm worried about the trolls. The ceremony is usually held in Troll Valley, but the clouds have been covering the Northern Lights here lately, so Grand Pabbie left to find a place where theyre still shining bright. Maybe we can find Grand Pabbie and help him locate a good spot for the ceremony this year.

Grand Pabbie

We just met Little Rock! He's like a little brother to Kristoff, and one of the young trolls hoping to participate in the Crystal Ceremony this year. He's very funny and sweet. Little Rock nearly knocked Kristoff over with a big hug when we arrived!

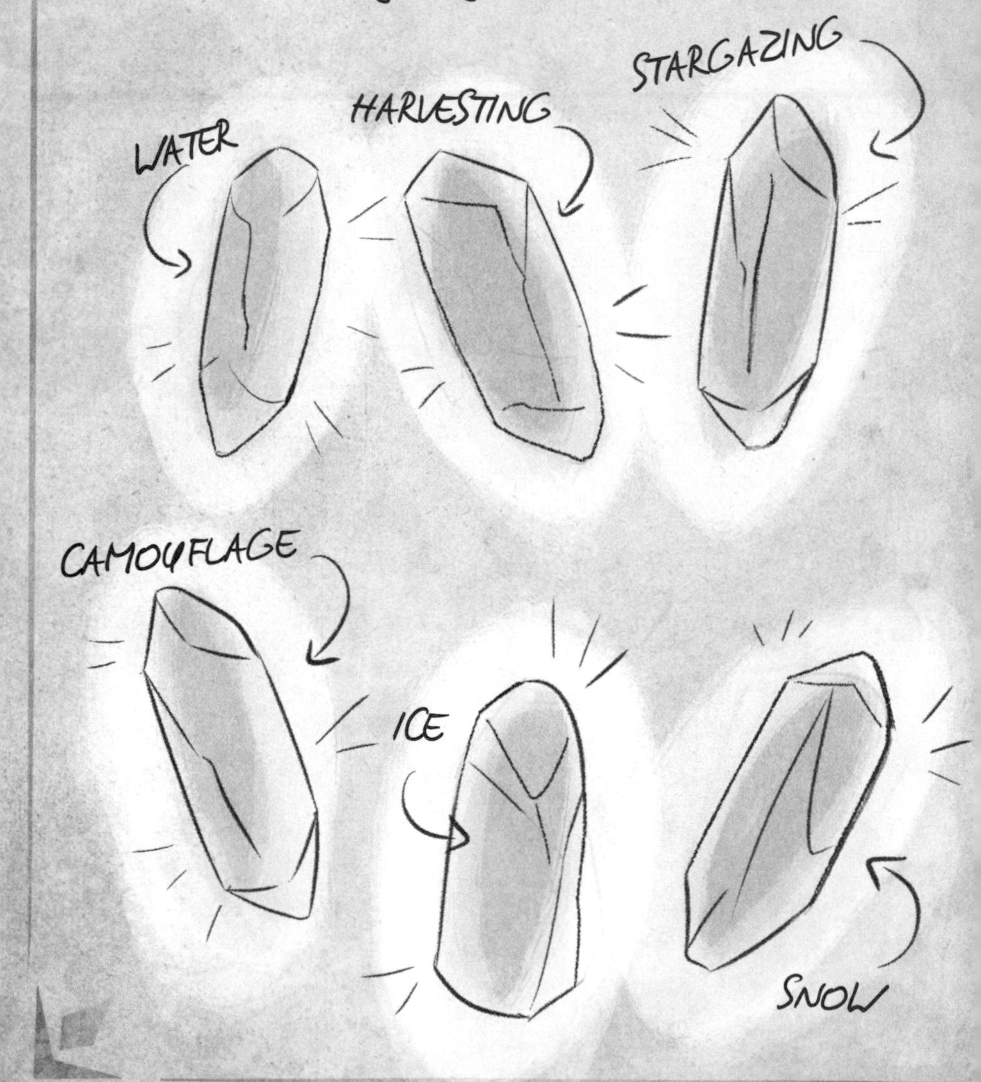

Little Rock has earned almost all his level-one crystals, and he keeps them in a small dark pouch.

But there's still one crystal he hasn't earned yet: his tracking crystal.

He has to earn it in the next three days or he can't be in the ceremony!

Once he earns it, it'll glow like the other crystals. So we're going to help him make it glow in time!

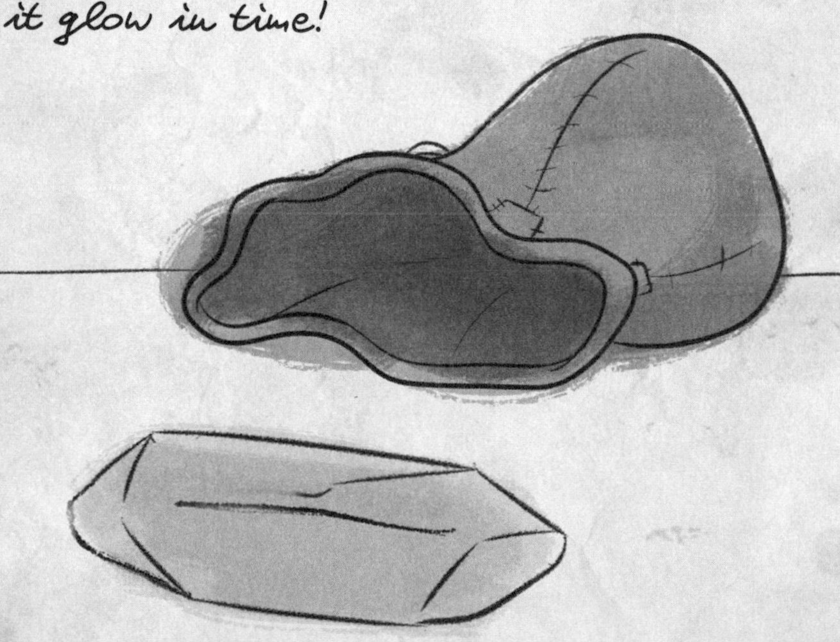

I'll be so proud to see Little Rock participate in the Crystal Ceremony. I've watched him grow up, and this is a big moment in every troll's life. All Little Rock has to do is earn that tracking crystal so it glows like all of his other level-one crystals. We all want to help him out!

I was already excited to be going to the Crystal Ceremony, but helping Little Rock earn his last level-one crystal will make it even more meaningful and special. Plus we have a new friend!

As the sun sets its sleepy head,
We trolls must wake from slumbering bed;
Our duties to the earth be made
Before the stars and moon do fade.

What Bulda just told us!

I'm not quite sure what this one means, either.

It means we travel at night.

So we'll have to sleep during the day like the trolls do! It's almost morning, and Little Rock needs to rest.

3 Nights Left

WE'RE about to SET off ON OUR QUEST to help Little Rock EARN his tracking crystal. WE only have tonight, tomorrow night, and the next night to do it.

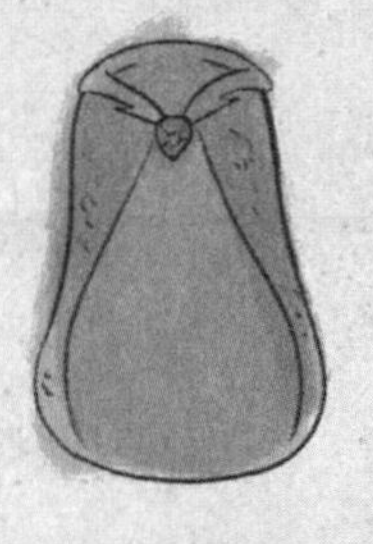
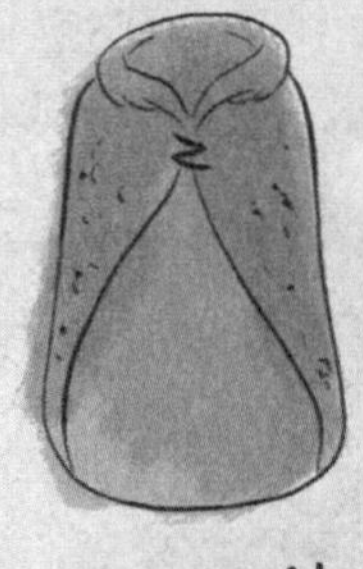

We said good-bye to Bulda and the other trolls, and she gave us these amazing mossy cloaks to keep us warm. Elsa didn't need one, of course. She loves the cold!

So, as Olaf said, "Let's go help Little Rock earn his tracking crystal!"

And we're off!

RULES OF TRACKING:

BE FEARLESS.

BE OBSERVANT.

BE INVENTIVE.

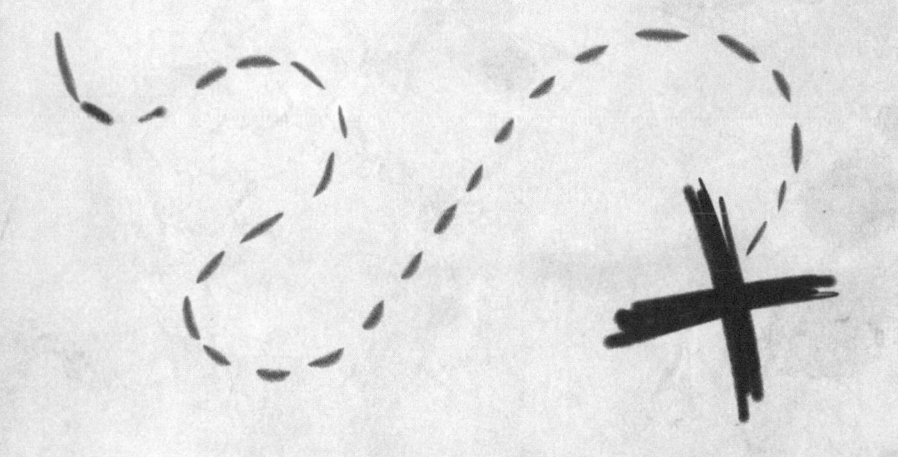

A TRUE ADVENTURE IS FULL OF SURPRISES.

We just left Troll Valley.
Little Rock is leading the way.
He might be even more excited than Anna!

I'm learning so much about troll tracking already!

Trolls sleep during the day, so we've been tracking at night. I love how bright the moon looks out here in the mountains. Olaf says the moon looks like a giant glowing snowball in the sky!

Who would have ever thought we'd be going on a nighttime tracking quest with a troll?!

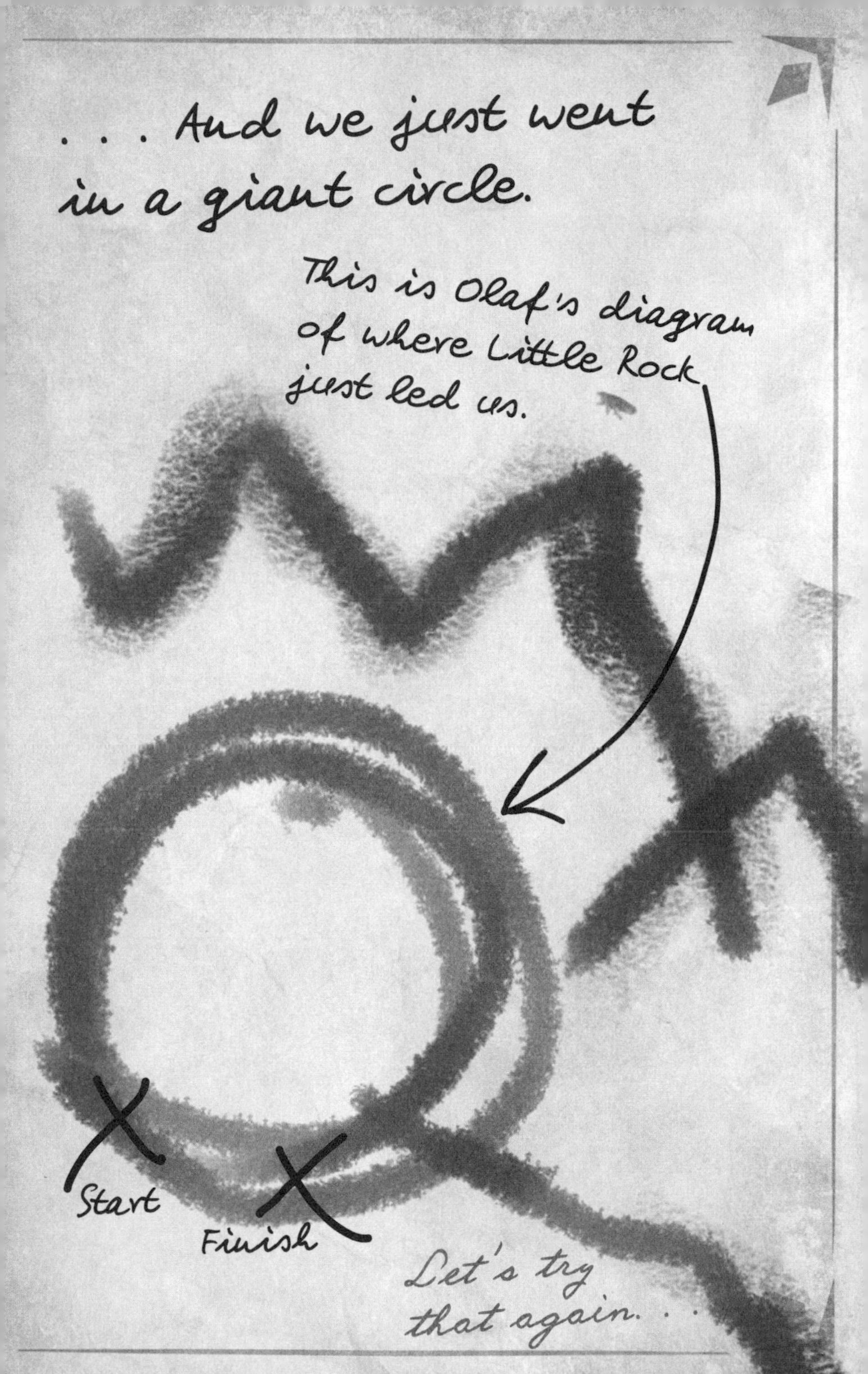
. . . And we just went in a giant circle.
This is Olaf's diagram of where Little Rock just led us.
Start
Finish
Let's try that again. . .

Little Rock has so many talents, but he definitely needs help when it comes to tracking. It doesn't come as naturally to him as it does to other trolls.

But the night sky is a great map. Trolls use the constellations to track where they are. Little Rock already has his level-one stargazing crystal! That should help him earn his tracking crystal, too.

I've read about the nocturnal animals that roam the forest at night, like owls, bats, and spiders. I really want to see a bat!

ANNA KEEPS THINKING SHE SEES ONE, BUT SO FAR IT'S ONLY BEEN FALLING LEAVES. WAIT, I THINK SHE JUST FOUND ONE!

Bats are amazing! I read that they have a special ability to sense things by reflecting sound. I wish we could get around in the dark just as easily as bats do.

Me too! I can tell Little Rock is getting nervous about earning his tracking crystal. But I know he can do it.

RULE OF TRACKING #1:

BE FEARLESS.

It's awfully cold, and we can hear wolves howling in the distance. It's a little eerie, but it's all part of the adventure! I know we can make it through anything together.

We've reached the top of the cliffs. Everyone cheered up when we saw a faint glimmer of the Northern Lights in the distance. I think Little Rock is leading us in the right direction!

We just came to a clearing
that divides into three paths.
Let's see which one
Little Rock takes!

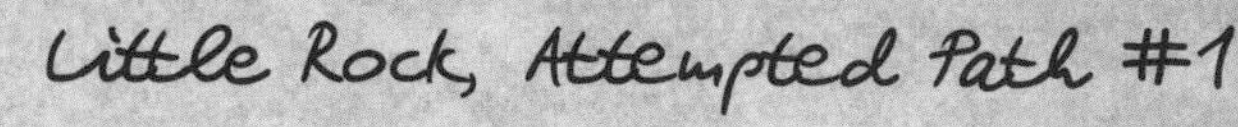

Little Rock, Attempted Path #1

This leads back to Troll Valley.

Little Rock, Attempted Path #2

This way will lead us back to Arendelle.

Little Rock, Attempted Path #3

I knew Little Rock would find the right path!

Trolls are excellent trackers. They know how to read the earth.

Usually.

Kristoff tells us that trolls have an incredible sense of smell.

Little Rock picked up a scent, but unfortunately, it led him straight to Sven. Olaf pointed out that at least we know Little Rock can help us find Sven if we ever lose him!

I'd NEVER lose SVEN!

"And I'd NEVER get lost!"

I think we should tell Little Rock a story to take his mind off things.

Elsa, we should write down our Northern Lights memory in here!

You're right! Want to start?

Okay, so growing up, Elsa and I loved the Northern Lights, but they were hard to see from the castle. We caught little glimpses here and there, but we always wanted to see them up close. Then one night, our parents tucked us into the carriage instead of tucking us into bed. Father drove us all the way to the foot of the mountain range, and we climbed up until we found a clearing in a beautiful meadow. Our parents sat down on a blanket, but Elsa and I couldn't sit still!

We ran all around the meadow together, jumping and scaring each other and playing games. We were having so much fun, we forgot all about the Northern Lights!

But then, out of nowhere, these amazing pink and green ribbons burst from the sky! I wanted to get closer, so I started running up a hill.

It was actually
an ice staircase
that I created!
We ran up and up until we couldn't
run anymore. Then we sat down at the
top, completely out of breath.

Oh, that must be one of my memories
of your magic that was changed! Anyway,
I remember we watched the Northern Lights
glow in the beautiful night sky together.

And we wished on them that we
would have more adventures together.

The night sky definitely heard our wish, because
a colorful snow flurry started to fall!

That was me, too.

It was a nice touch.

I'm glad you liked it.

Shoes for Valking on the Snov

Racket

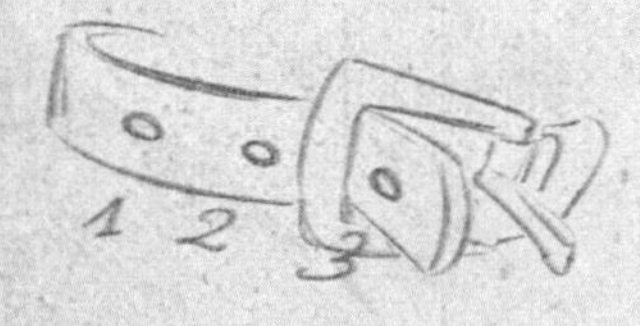

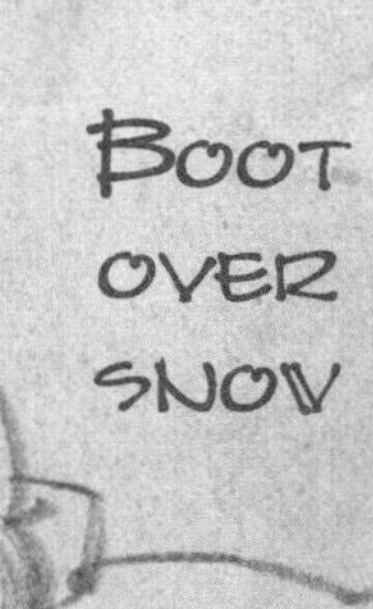

PREVENT SINKING IN THE SNOW.

UNNECESSARY.

Agreed! I like the feeling of snow on my feet.

Well, I could use a pair right now!

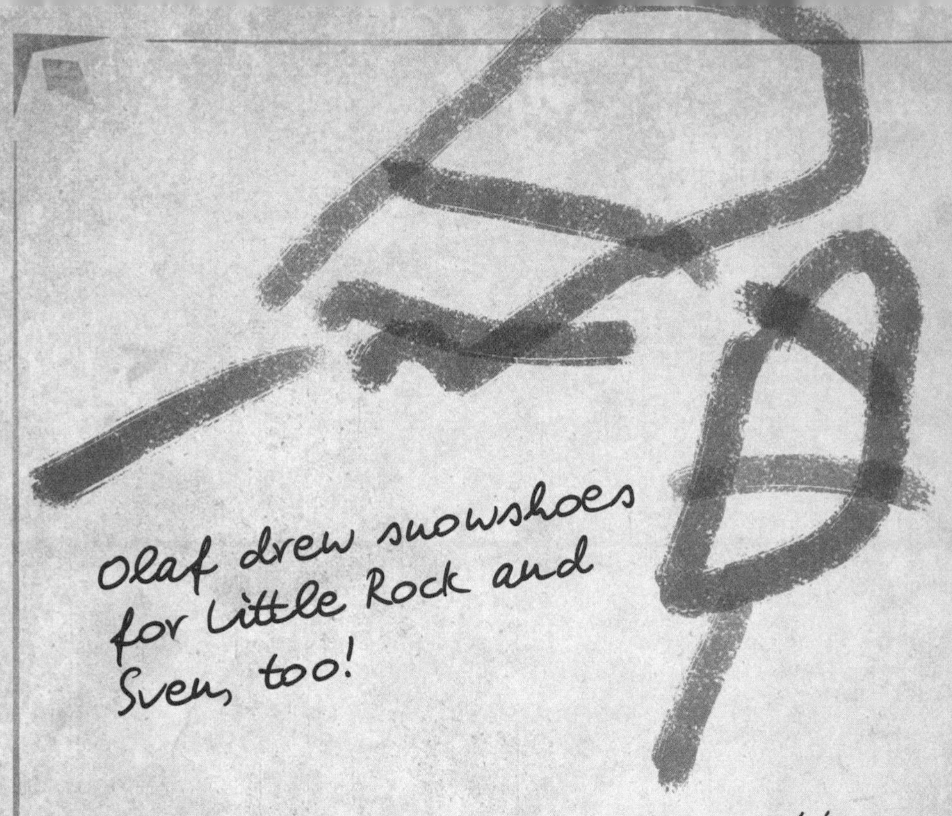

We've finally reached the top of the mountain, where the ground is level.

There's a frozen river ahead. Our plan is to walk slowly and look out for thin ice.

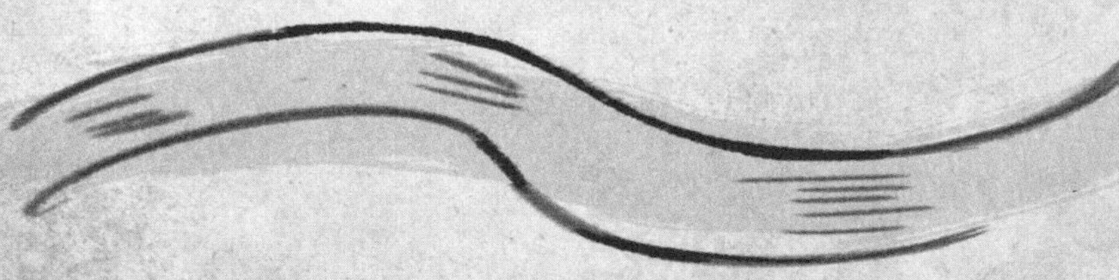

We'll have to tread carefully. . .

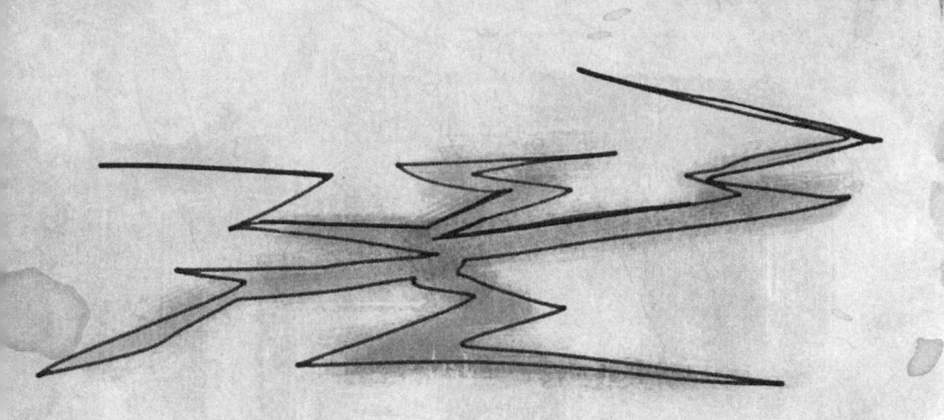

When Little Rock skipped onto the ice, it cracked!

Kristoff and I grabbed him right before he fell into the freezing cold water. Now how will we cross the river to get to safety?

I guess those snow-walking shoes would be useful now. . .

Anna had the idea for me to make a staircase out of ice to get us across the river, but the riverbank beneath the staircase crumbled! I quickly made ice sleds to help us glide across the frozen river.

It was a bit scary and it could have been a dissster, but we worked together and made it across safely!

And Olaf said it was the best ride ever.

Elsa's magic was amazing!
That was some quick thinking
in a slippery situation!

Little Rock presented his ice crystal to Elsa and me for our fearlessness on the frozen river. It was so generous of him to share his hard-earned ice crystal with us! Little Rock is full of kindness and love.

Yes, we will take good care of this ice crystal for Little Rock until he needs it for the ceremony!

After all that excitement, we decided it was a good time to set up camp for the night. We are next to a brook watching the sun rise above us. It reminds me of my childhood with the trolls. We used to watch the sunrise every morning before we all fell asleep.

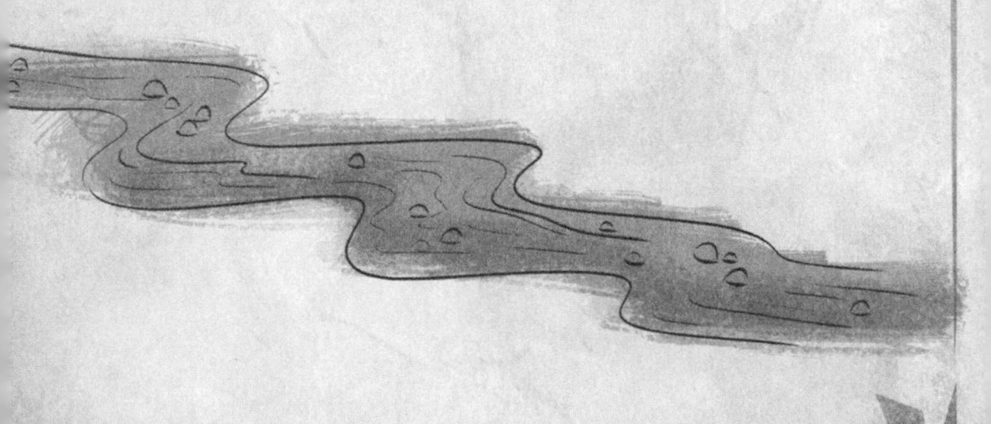

Sun Balm

Reflects the sun's rays

Apply generously!

GOOD FOR EVERYONE

WON'T WORK FOR SNOWMEN

Kristoff just told me and Anna that if Little Rock doesn't earn the tracking crystal in time, he will have to wait another year to be in the Crystal Ceremony. Little Rock would be so devastated if that happened. I really hope we can help him!

We only have two nights left before the ceremony. I hate to think of Little Rock being left out. I know it would break his heart. We will start tracking again as soon as we wake up.

RULE OF TRACKING #2:

BE OBSERVANT.

2 Nights Left

We are back on Grand Pabbie's trail, with Little Rock in the lead. Tonight he is going to work on the second rule of tracking: being observant! He's searching the area for clues, and he just found a branch! This could lead to something!

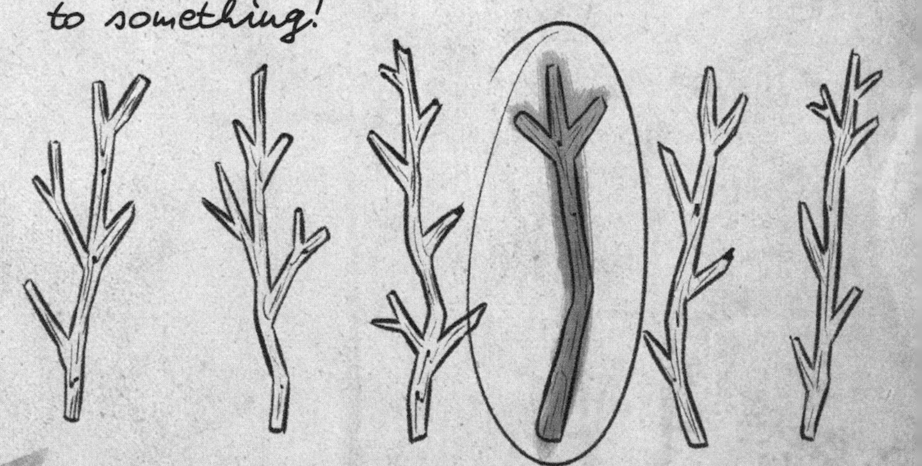

Never mind, it was just Olaf's arm. It wasn't a clue, but Olaf sure was happy to have his arm back!

Little Rock just has to keep trying. He'll find a real clue somewhere.

The Northern Lights disappeared again, much to our disappointment. There are beautifully bright stars, however. I don't think I've ever seen so many. Olaf told Little Rock that the stars sleep during the day and wake up and sparkle at night just like the trolls.

Speaking of Little Rock, he just found a piece of moss. He thought it might belong to Grand Pabbie's cloak, but it was just a regular piece of moss like the kind lining the trail.

Olaf wanted
me to put a
sample in here.

Kit for Mending of Clothes

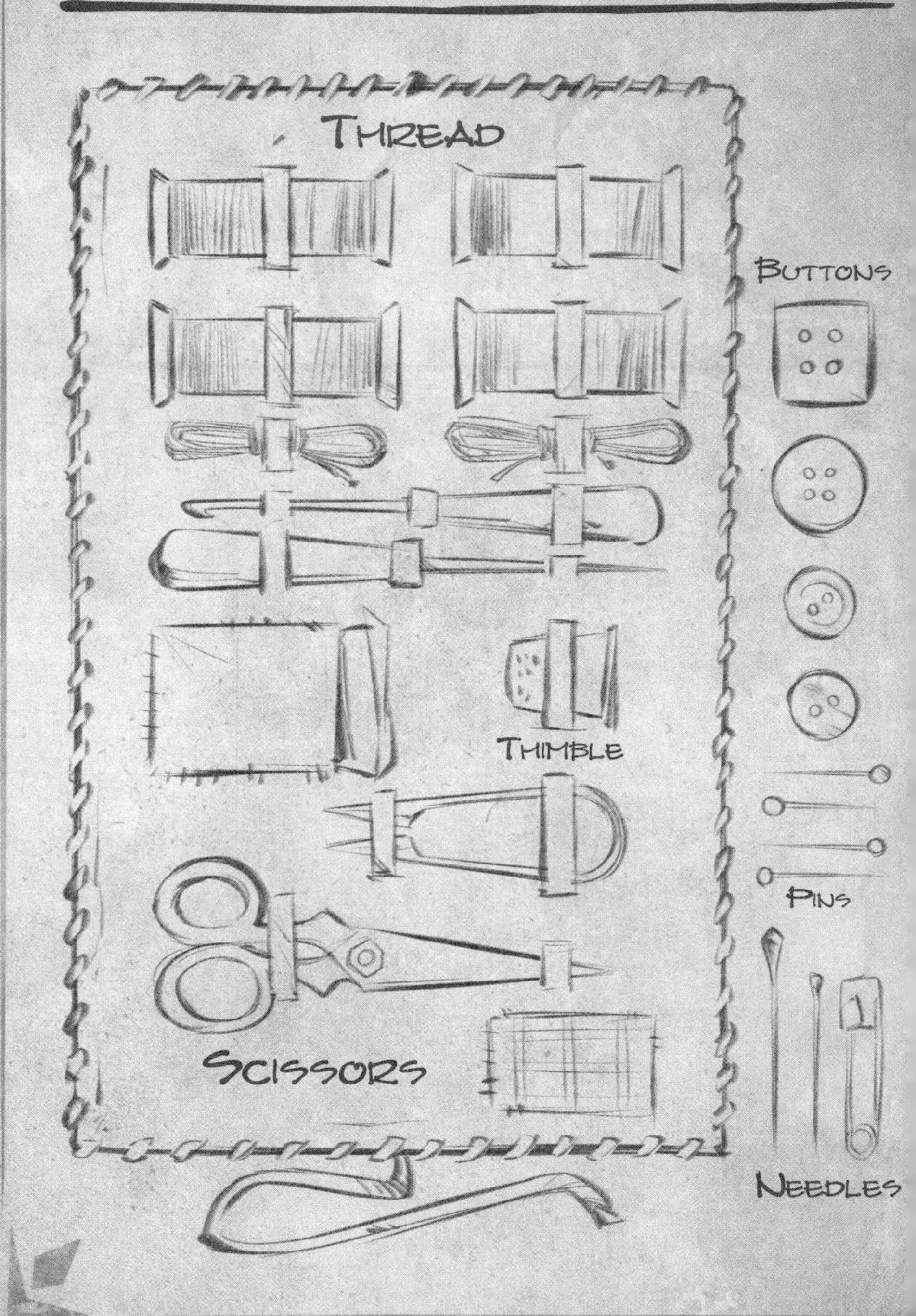

KIT CAN ROLL AND UNROLL.

EASY TO CARRY

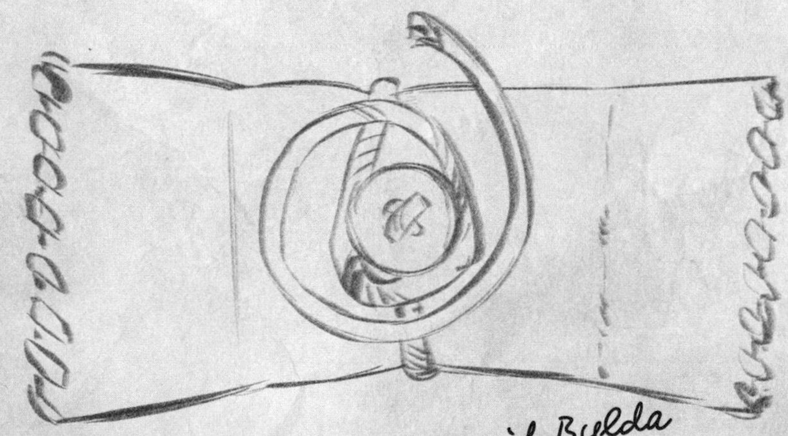

LIGHTWEIGHT I wonder if Bulda could use one of these for her mossy cloaks. . .

Little Rock found another clue, and it's a good one—footprints! Me and Sven see paw prints a lot out in the forest. Once, they led us right to a snacking bear cub . . . and its mother bear. . . . That was an exciting day. . . .

Anyway, let's see where these prints lead. . . .

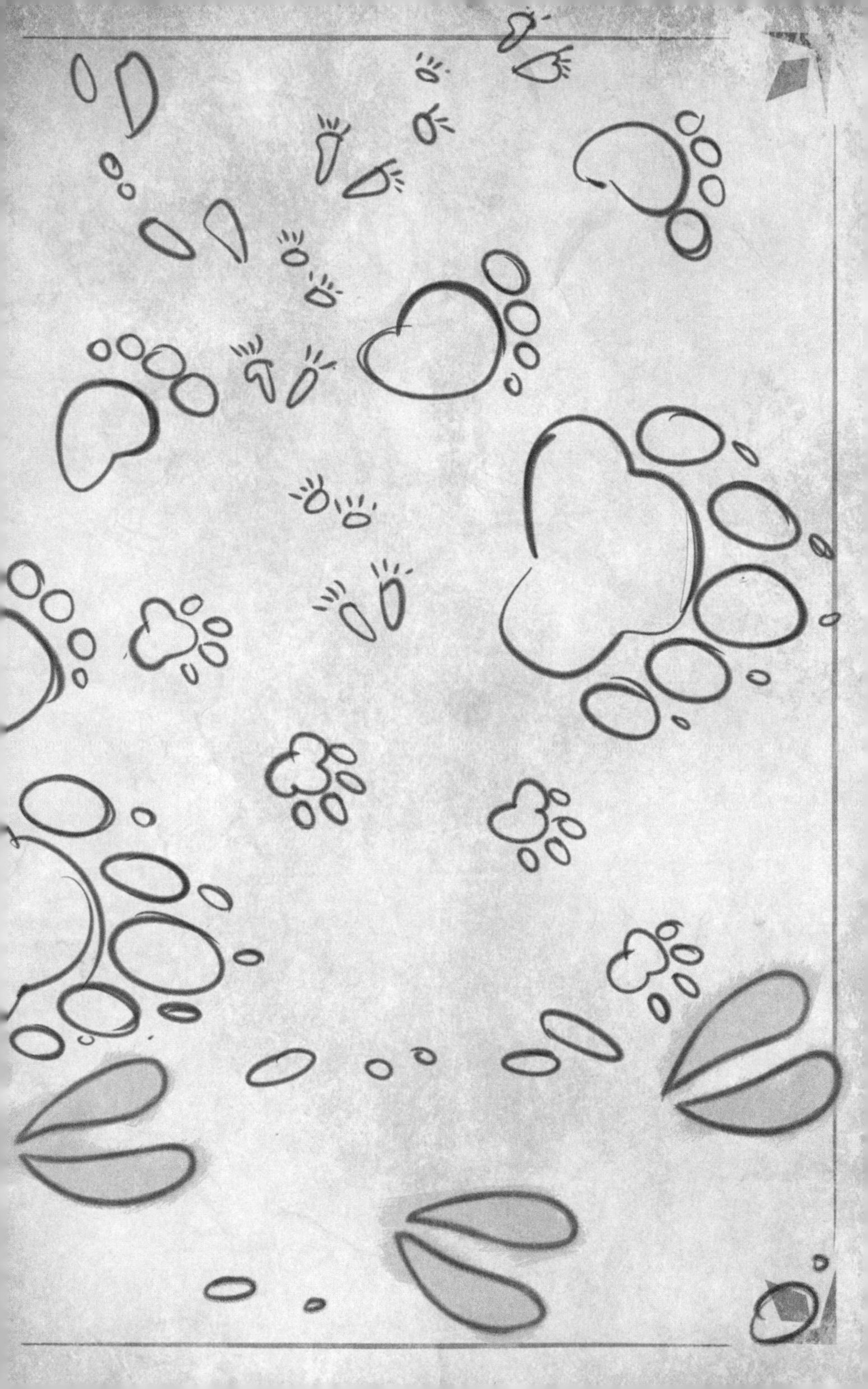

They led us right to Sven! It might be hard to find Grand Pabbie, but Sven says, "Little Rock is very good at finding me!"

That's true, he is!

Kristoff and I asked Little Rock to look at the prints again since he knows Grand Pabbie the best. Judging by the size of <u>these</u> prints, they really could be his tracks!

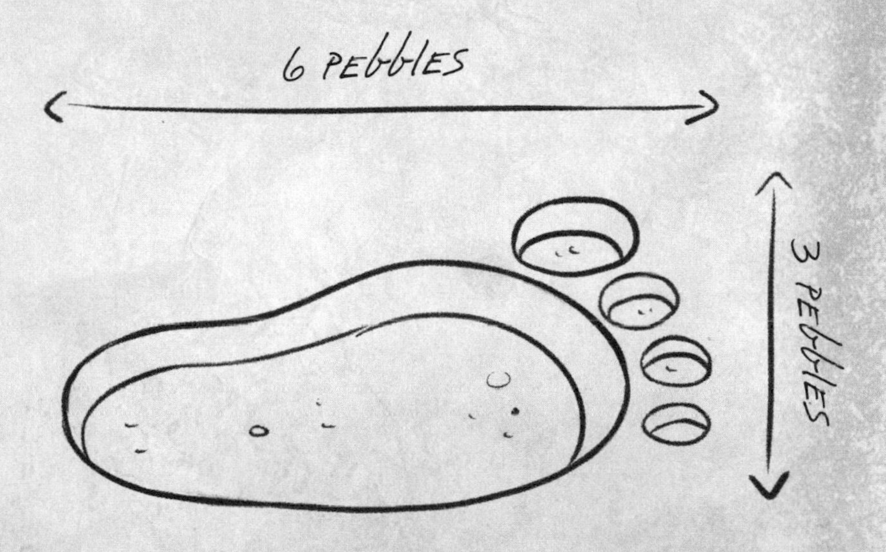

This could be exactly the clue Little Rock needs! We're going to follow them to see where they go. . . .

The prints led to a precipice,
but then they just . . . ended!
What could have happened?

Little Rock is really worried.

Uh-oh. A dark cloud has just covered the stars, and it seems to be growing bigger. It looks like a storm is coming. The wind is picking up! We need to find shelter—quick!

We didn't have time to find shelter, so I used my magic to quickly create one.

ELSA REALLY IS AN ARTIST WITH ICE.

Thanks, Kristoff. It's nice to be safe inside here together!

Elsa built the coziest ice shelter to shield us from the storm. It's curved at the top and thick enough to keep us safe. As we were waiting for the storm to end, Olaf told his own Northern Lights story. He said that the first time he saw the Northern Lights was the night that Elsa created him. He had just learned how to walk and talk, when suddenly he began tumbling down a mountain. He lost all of his parts. He looked at a bird for guidance on how to put himself back together. Now that's observant! After the bird flew away, Olaf noticed the bright green Northern Lights glowing in the night sky. What a wonderful memory!

Sven says, "Olaf's story made me forget about the storm." Me too. Looks like it's over!

I wonder what we should do next. I don't want to worry anyone, but the snow is going to make tracking harder. Any prints that might have been on the ground will be gone by now.

We can't give up.

Grand Pabbie must have traveled down the other side of the mountain. Maybe there's another clue down there for Little Rock to find!

At first, we didn't know how to get down the mountain. But Olaf said it reminded him of the mountain in his story, which gave Little Rock the idea that we should roll down it.

When we reached the bottom, Little Rock gave Olaf his snow crystal for helping to come up with the idea to roll down the mountain. Little Rock might not be the best at tracking, but he's a great friend.

It was observant of Little Rock to use Olaf's story as a way to get down the mountain. I'd say he mastered the second rule of tracking! He also made Olaf very happy. The little guy can't stop hugging his new snow crystal.

Right when we
thought
we were safe at
the bottom of
the mountain, an
avalanche started!
is jus
back! I'm
it safe for
ack to Arendelle,
uvent pockets for
hat's more of an

We got stuck in the snow, and pieces of rock and ice were falling around us! Anna saw an overhang, so we rushed toward it. We barely made it in time!

We thought for sure the avalanche was going to sweep us up and I might have to use my magic again, but the snow shot right over the rocky ledge. Anna's smart thinking saved us. This adventure really has been full of surprises!

Olaf thought he lost his snow crystal in the avalanche, but it was just stuck in his back! I'm going to keep it safe for him. Maybe when we get back to Arendelle, I can ask Oaken to invent pockets for snowmen. Or maybe that's more of an Elsa question.

Avalanche Invention Ideas

~~Avalanche Wall~~

~~Avalanche Port~~

~~Avalanche Sleigh~~

~~Run~~

Never mind.
Stay at home and take a sauna.

With all the excitement, we lost track of time! The sun is rising slowly in the distance, casting orange-yellow light over the horizon. I can't believe how beautiful it is up here. We're going to camp out and rest beneath the overhang. Everyone will feel refreshed after a good night's (or, rather, day's) sleep. Time to give Kristoff and Elsa a turn to write in here before bed.

Let's see . . . Autumn is almost over, and winter is swiftly on its way. I'm concerned about Little Rock. I know he will be heartbroken if he doesn't earn his tracking crystal in time for this year's ceremony. And we only have one night left before the big event. Where could Grand Pabbie be??

I'm worried about Little Rock, too. So many things need to happen in such a short time. We need the Northern Lights to be brighter, we need to find Grand Pabbie, and Little Rock's tracking crystal needs to glow.

SVEN AGREES.

It's been an incredible night full of adventures, and everyone is tired. In fact, the sun's barely up and Little Rock is already fast asleep!

The Stove for the

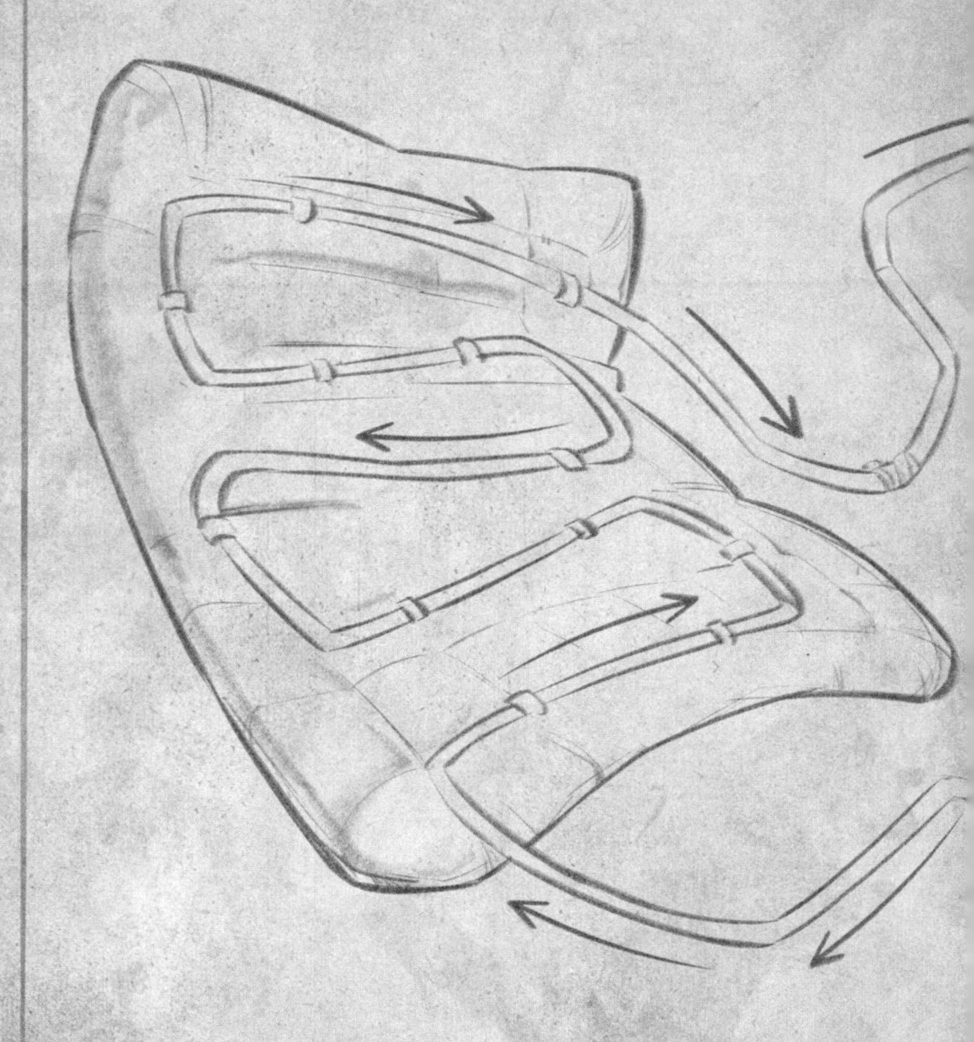

Good for snuggling.
Keeps family cozy.

Heating of Blankets

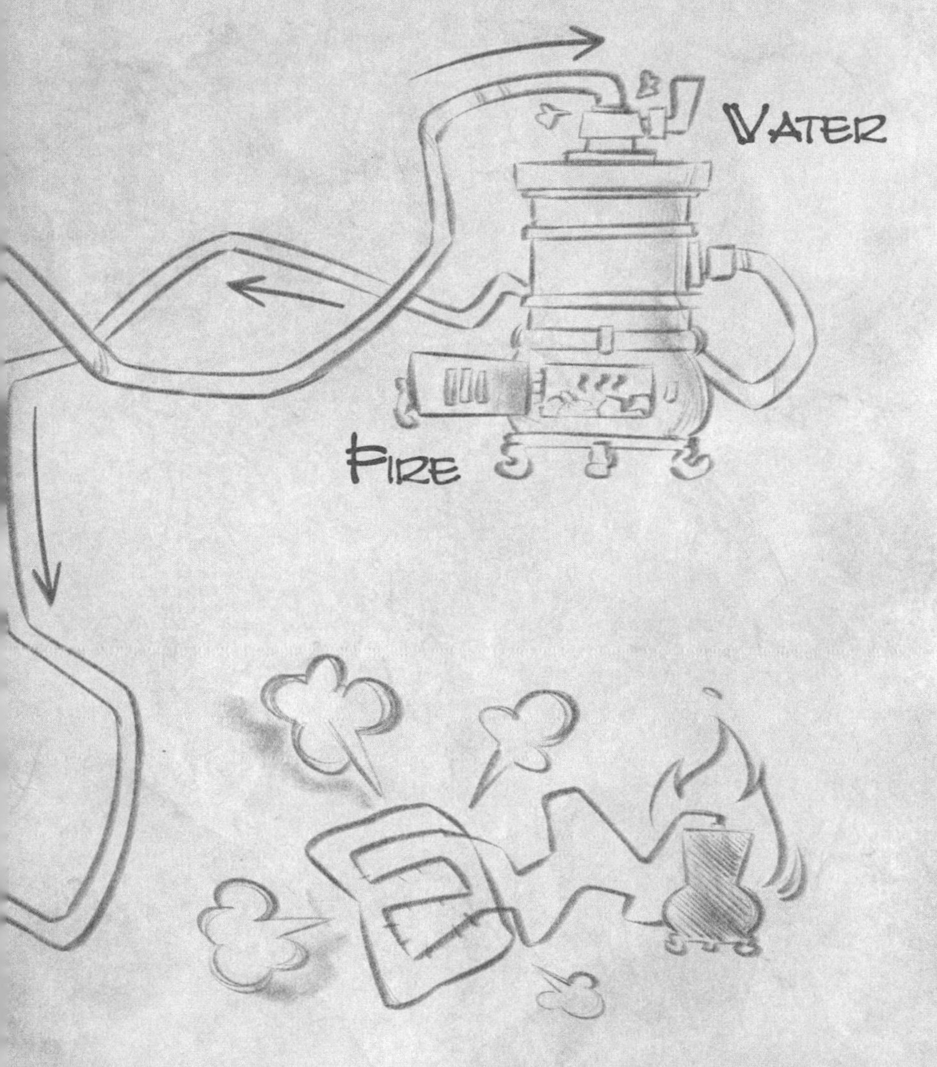

Important: Be careful not to get burned.

I have no idea why anyone would need this.

Night of Crystal Ceremony

Little Rock just woke everyone up! We slept all day, and now it's dark out. I'm glad we all got some rest, but we have to find Grand Pabbie before the sun rises. That only gives us a few more hours! We'll start down the lower mountain trail. It looks like the snow thins out toward the bottom.

RULE OF TRACKING #3:

BE INVENTIVE.

The third rule of tracking is being inventive. It reminds me of my own Northern Lights memory. One night, when Sven was just a little guy, we were out harvesting our ice. The sky was clear and the Northern Lights were right above us. The colors were reflected all over the ice, which was driving Sven crazy! He kept trying to catch the light, but every time he put down his hoof, the light would move somewhere else.

It was pretty funny to watch. That is, until he tried to catch the light with his tongue—and he got stuck to the ice!

I tried everything I could to free him. I pulled. I pushed. Nothing was working. So I had to be inventive. I grabbed an ice pick and—chip, chip, chip—carved off the piece of ice that Sven's tongue was stuck to. He was a little nervous at first, but it worked! That little piece of ice melted in his mouth. After that, we sat down and watched the Northern Lights together. It was a perfect night. Isn't that right, buddy?

"You sure are clever, Kristoff."

watch. T

until he trie

to catch

the light

with his

tongue—

and he got

stuck to

the ice!

"That ice tasted delicious.
Almost as good as this paper.
But not as good as carrots . . ."

Even though we are on a mission to help Little Rock, and time is running out, it is lovely being in the mountains together. We've been walking for quite a while. We just turned a corner and found a giant waterfall.

Wow!!

And we found a clue—a piece of Grand Pabbie's cloak! Kristoff says if his cloak is here, then he must have found a way up the waterfall. But how?

Sven figured it out.
He licked the water.

We thought he was just thirsty, but it turned out he was trying to tell us something!

"If the water was frozen, we could climb it."

Great idea, Sven!
I'll freeze the waterfall.

He's a genius, that reindeer. What would I do without him?

LIFTER-UPPER

GOOD FOR THE SCALING OF CLIFFS.

We are going to climb the frozen waterfall!

USE SUPER-STRONG ROPE.

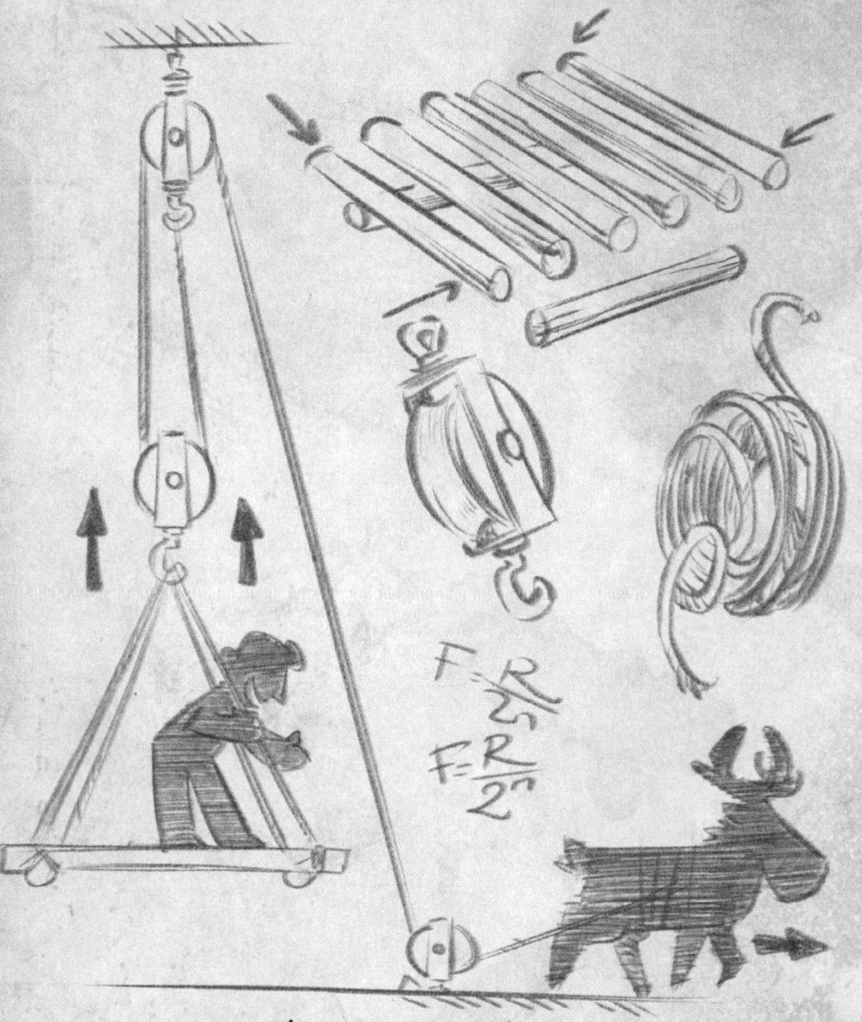

I knew we'd need Oaken's "special super-strong" rope for something!

Anna is so excited to climb the waterfall. She's not afraid of anything!

Race you to the top!

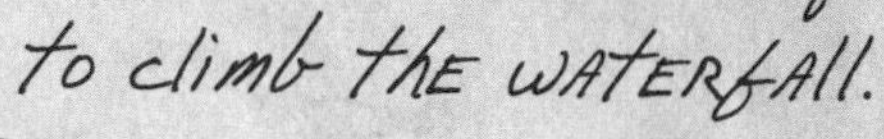

ANNA NEEDED SOME EQUIPMENT to climb THE WATERFALL.

I could have made it without it.

THE EQUIPMENT HELPED.

All right, the equipment helped. And I am pretty good with an ice ax.

YOU'RE AMAZING WITH AN ICE AX.

I climbed a waterfall!

It's a good thing we have Oaken's super-strong rope to help the others up.

WELL . . .

You're telling me that you can pull Sven up the waterfall without Oaken's rope?

OKAY, OKAY. WE'LL TRY THE ROPE.

We threw the rope down to Elsa. She made a sling around Sven and put Olaf between his antlers. Then we pulled them up!

Little Rock was next. He was even heavier than Sven. Trolls weigh a lot, but we pulled hard, and he was really brave! I could tell he was proud of himself for making it all the way to the top, and I'm proud of him, too.

I GUESS OAKEN'S ROPE REALLY WAS SUPER STRONG!

I created steps up the waterfall to get myself to the top. I would have made them earlier, but I knew Anna wouldn't want to miss out on climbing up a waterfall with an ice ax! Plus, it was funny to see Kristoff's face when he realized I was already up there with them.

Did I mention that I climbed a waterfall?

Little Rock gave his water crystal to Sven for being inventive!

Sven was really smart to think of freezing the waterfall, but I hope Little Rock knows that we will always help him no matter what. He's family!

Plus he saved my life many years ago!

Wait, what?

All right, here's the story:

Sven and I were in Troll Valley celebrating Bulda's birthday with everyone. The young trolls, including Little Rock, were learning about plants. I was really hungry (as usual), so I sat down to have a snack.

Suddenly, Little Rock jumped up and knocked the sandwich right out of my mouth! It turned out that it had the leaves of a tysbast plant in it. Trolls can eat them, but theyre deadly to humans. I wouldn't be here if it wasn't for him.

Thank you, Little Rock!

Kristoff says trolls use poems to learn about plants. Here are a few examples:

Rock tripe be tasty when
crunchy and dry,
but after a rainfall you may slip
and fly.

Three-lobed clover is best
for colds,
but four and five lobes
are good to rid molds.

I like this one.

DO NOT EAT!
The tysbast leaves be good
for a troll,
but humans who eat them pay
quite a toll.
I'LL NEVER FORGET
THIS ONE!

Little Rock just told us, "This has been the best adventure I've ever been on and I've made all these great new friends. Whether we make it or not, that's all that matters!"

We agree, but we still want him to earn his crystal! He's worked so hard and come so far and shown so much bravery! We can't give up now.

Elsa's right. And we only have a few more hours left of autumn! The sun will be rising soon.

We need to pick up the pace. Let's run to the top of the trail!

Anna loves to go fast. And she can't resist a challenge. As she took off, she shouted: "Last one to the top is a rotten herring!" I love her sense of humor and her sense of adventure!

Made it to the top! And I have to say, there is nothing quite as funny as seeing Sven run full speed up a hill with Olaf in his antlers.

The fog at the top of the trail is really dense. It is really hard to see anything. . . .

A Vessel for the

When it's darkest night . . .

LIGHTING OF THE WAY

This seems useful, but I'm pretty sure Oaken is the only person who could carry this lantern through a forest.

I think I see something up ahead. . . .

We found Grand Pabbie!!!

Oh, dear. Little Rock just ran up and hugged a rock that looked like Grand Pabbie instead of the actual Grand Pabbie. We pointed him in the right direction.

It feels just like a family reunion. Let's see if Little Rock earned his tracking crystal!

Oh, no! Little Rock's tracking crystal still isn't glowing. What could be the matter???

Could something be wrong with the crystal?

Poor Little Rock! I hope he's not discouraged!

Little Rock has gone through so much to get here.

Little Rock just admitted to us that he's not very good at tracking, and that he would never have found Grand Pabbie on his own.

Then he said, "If anyone here has earned a tracking crystal, it's all of you. I needed you, my friends, to get here. I may not be a great tracker, but I do have great friends."

And then . . . Little Rock's crystal lit up! It's glowing! He did it!

Grand Pabbie said that the crystals shine when a troll gains the skills necessary to be successful. Because Little Rock realized that he needed help from his friends to learn how to track, his crystal lit up. He has all his level-one crystals now!

Little Rock's heart always leads him in the right direction, even if the rest of him gets a little lost.

All the other young trolls who earned their level-one crystals just jumped out of hiding. They've been waiting for Little Rock all along!

The Northern Lights are shimmering faintly, so Grand Pabbie is going to do the Crystal Ceremony right here.

Olaf's right: this is going to be the best ceremony ever!

GRAND PABBIE FOUND THE PERFECT PLACE TO HAVE THE CRYSTAL CEREMONY. THE NORTHERN LIGHTS ARE RIGHT ABOVE US.

We are so honored to be here!

We knew Little Rock could do it!

We thanked Little Rock for lending us his crystals, and gave them back to him. He needs them for the Crystal Ceremony—which is starting right now!

The trolls are holding their crystals up to the night sky, and the Northern Lights are reflecting off them. All the pinks and greens and blues in the sky are there, but Grand Pabbie says he wishes the colors were even brighter.

I think I may be able to help. . . .

Elsa just sent a giant snowflake into the air that made the lights beam in every direction. Left, right, front, back, up, down. It was incredible! We were all covered in colors!

I've been to a lot of Crystal Ceremonies, but this one is extra special. I'm so happy to be here with Anna, Elsa, Olaf, Sven, and the rest of my family.

The trolls just held their crystals up one last time. Elsa's snowflake is still twirling above everyone. The lights are the brightest I've ever seen them and only growing brighter!

Everyone in Troll Valley will know Little Rock has earned his tracking crystal now!

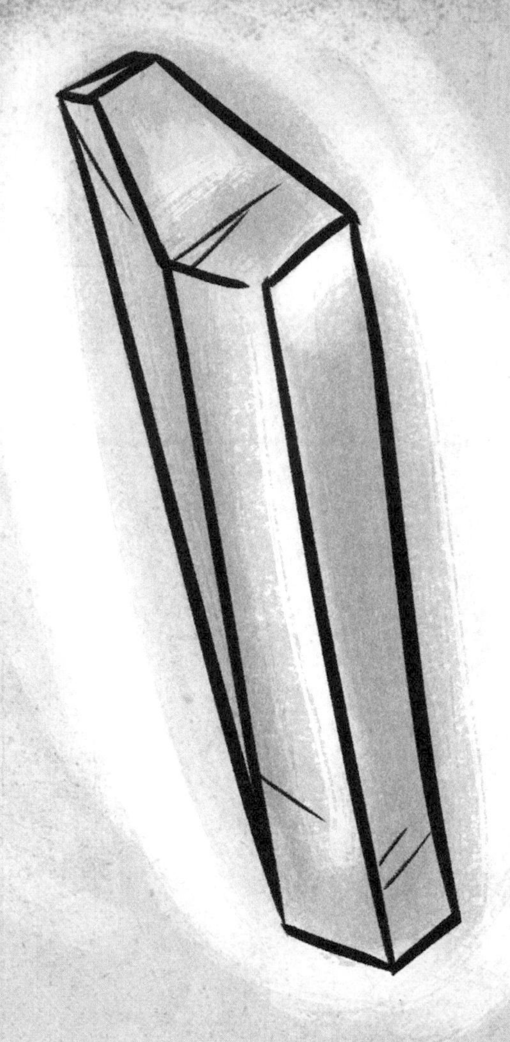

Grand Pabbie just reminded us that the crystals represent the connection trolls have with nature. He said . . . a little help again, Kristoff?

For trolls, this is the beginning of a lifelong responsibility to nurture both the earth and sky.

The trolls must do their part to make the crystals glow, and in turn, those crystals help keep the Northern Lights alive.

Then, all together, the trolls said:

We Guardians of earth do know
Autumn lights and crystals glow
So our bond may deepen and grow.

Oh, I kind of understand now!

Me too!

The trolls depend on nature, so they take care of it.

Exactly!

I've always loved the Northern Lights, but now I realize how important they are to the trolls, our kingdom, and the earth. I'm glad we kept this notebook for the castle library! That was a good idea, Anna!

This is so much more than a record for the castle library. It's proof that we had a true adventure. It was really special hearing everyone's Northern Lights stories. The lights have played a big part in all our lives, and now they've brought us even closer together.

Yeah, it's going to be pretty hard to top this Northern Lights memory.

I guess we'll just have to come back next year and try.

How did I know you were going to say that?

Olaf's painting of the Northern Lights!

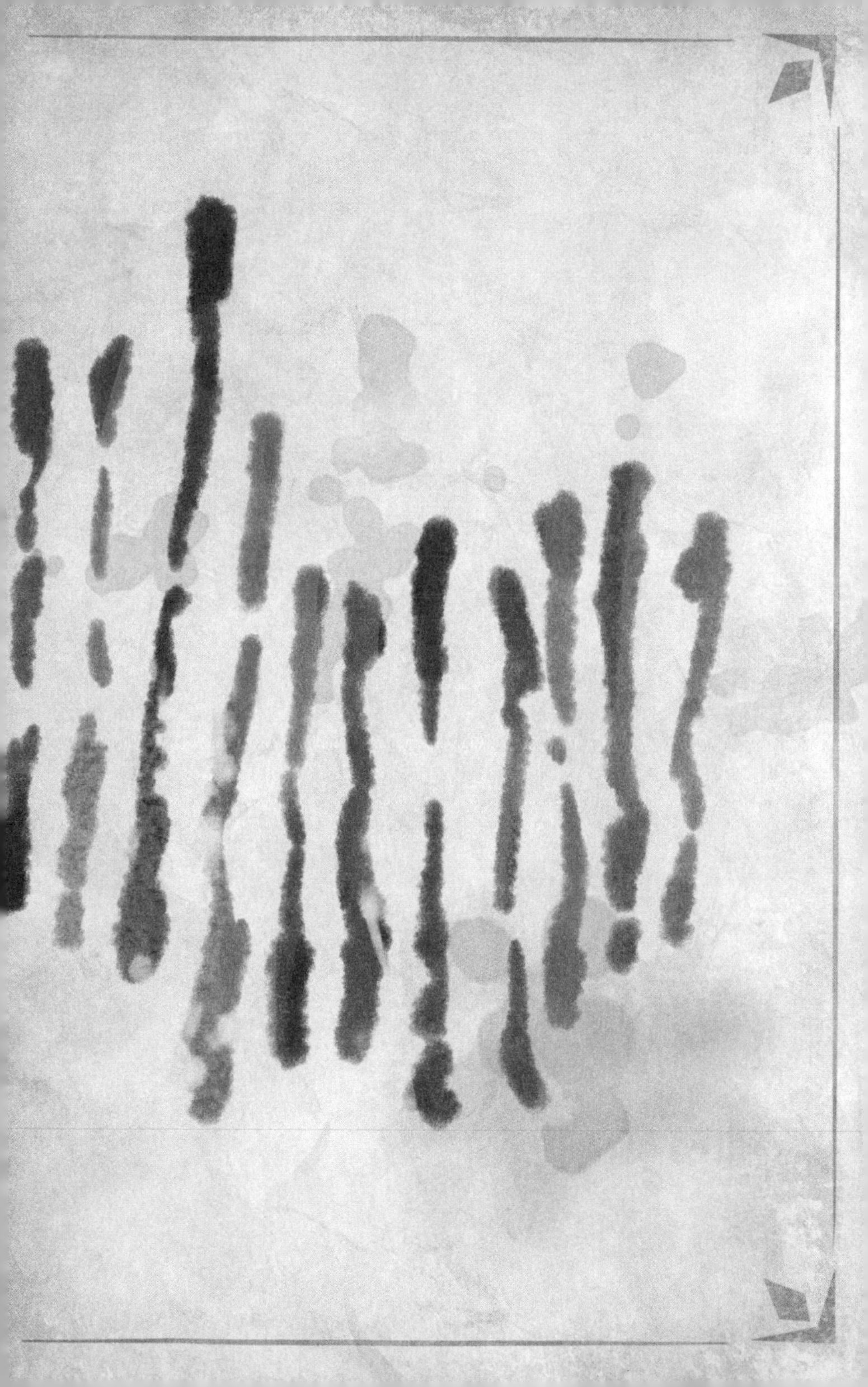

The Crystal Ceremony is over. We're on our way back to Arendelle!

We were sad to say good-bye to Little Rock, but we know our paths will cross again soon!

I can't wait to add this notebook to the Arendelle library, so the kingdom can learn from Little Rock!

The fact that he earned his tracking crystal shows that anything can be achieved. . .

This true adventure taught me so much, like the importance of being fearless . . .

being observant . . .

and
being
inventive.

It also helps to have really good friends! Isn't that right, Sven?

"That's
the most
important
part,
Kristoff."

AND REMEMBER, A TRUE ADVENTURE
is full of SURPRISES.

Our journey to the
Northern Lights was a
great surprise, Kristoff.

Yes, it was! I can't wait for
our next adventure together!

Adventure NOTEBOOK

160 Pages

AN INVENTION PERFECT FOR RECORDING OTHER INVENTIONS.

FRIENDS + FEARLESS, OBSERVANT, AND INVENTIVE = SUCCESS!

Elsa

Kristoff

Anna

N
W
E
S
©Disney

Sun Balm

Shoes for Walking on the Snow

Kit for Mending of Clothes

Brand-New Super-Strong Rope!
of my own invention

Arendelle

Stove for the Heating of Blankets

Vessel for the Lighting of the Way

I could USE A SAUNA.

Let's all go
have a sauna!

Race you there!